CUP OF COLD WATER

CUP OF COLD WATER

POEMS AND PHOTOGRAPHS BY

SIV CEDERING FOX

NEW RIVERS PRESS

1973

poems and photographs copyright © 1973 by siv cedering fox
library of congress catalog card number 73-76236
isbn 0-912284-47-1 (cloth)
      0-912284-46-3 (paper)

book design by robin fox

thanks to the editors and publishers of the following magazines for permission to reprint poems and photographs that originally appeared in their publications:

ANTAEUS, BLACK BOX, CHICAGO TRIBUNE, CRAZY HORSE, DRYAD, THE FALCON, FIRST ISSUE, LAND AT THE TIP OF A HAIR (poems in woodcut by wang hui-ming), MEASURE, MILL MOUNTAIN REVIEW, NEW YORK QUARTERLY, QUARTERLY REVIEW OF LITERATURE, SATURDAY REVIEW, SUMAC, and VOYAGES

distributed in great britain   philip spender
                                  69 randolph avenue
                                  london, w9, england

in the united states and elsewhere by:

                                  serendipity books
                                  1790 shattuck avenue
                                  berkeley, california
                                  94709

this book was manufactured in the united states of america for new rivers press, p.o. box 578, cathedral station, new york, n.y. 10025 in a first edition of 1200 copies, of which 900 have been bound in paper, 300 in cloth with 30 of the latter signed and numbered by the author.

I. THE CUP

I light the stove
in the empty house;
a fly awakens.

I laugh at myself.

I had come to be alone.

CUP OF COLD WATER

I

I scoop a bucket
full of snow,

heap the whiteness
in a bowl
and set it by the stove,

that we can wash
our hands.

I fill the bucket
full again

to melt:
a small amount

for us
to drink.

II

When we have slept
the measure of the night,

we wash our hands,
break the bread
and lift our cups.
You say:

this water lacks
the journey through the earth,
the taste of soil
and rock.

It has traveled
only through the air.
What good is heaven
in a lover's cup?

III

The snow is coming down.

We open the door
to look
and let the cold
come in.

I say: In summer
when the snow is rain,
I will put the bucket out
and fill it full
that I can wash my hair
with rain.

You cup my face.
You say:

IV

In the spring I bend to drink.
The brook is full of melting things.

My two hands form a broken cup
to hold the taste of
granite, moss,
a trace of
rabbit, grouse.

I cup my hands to drink again
— water falls
full of hooves
of moose, and deer.
The vessel of my fingers spills

the print of weasel and of quail,
and as sun breaks over rock,
mountains melt and river
in my mouth.

THE POEM OF THE CUP

I

walk through things
familiar
trees and
parting
branches

come upon a brook
dark and narrow
slit
of water

watch your step
upon the stones

. . .

turn the light out
in the room
the room is snow

look deep
into that water

someplace further on
it is river
shores you walked
the curves of
women

and still further on
it is sea
lifting
to the moon

I could come to you
as water

. . .

the cup was broken
you can mend it
you have travelled
up the river

you have recognized
the silence

you have skipped the stone
watched the breaking
of the surface
circle
circle

to the mountains
that give speed
and sound

        I want to name you

to your hands

        but the whiteness
        overwhelms I cannot
        say your name

lips and water lick your hands
I cannot

        Say your name

II

I go out into the night
cup my hands
as if to drink
cold water
from a brook

I hold them up
let them fill
with night

I hold the night
I try
to drink

. . .

I spread my arms
as if diving the swan
into the night

I close my eyes
and dive

. . .

and with my arms still spread
I lie down

all the space
above the cross of my body
widens
outward
endlessly

I hold that space:
moons
nebula
as night spills
out of my hands:

the broken cup

. . .

I want to name
parts of my body:
forhead
lips
breasts
belly
thighs

this space
this space
I could give you
this space

III

this is a cold
country
here you believe
in flesh

the cold
reminds you

. . .

          my hand in cold
waters
remember
fire

          my face in the falling
snow
burns

. . .

on the narrow bed
I will think
of the first night
of winter

close to the fire:

I became
a brook

your tongue
on pebbles

your hands
made me water

your lips
drank

14

IV

This is the poem of the cup
It takes me to a white country

I live in a small house
tend a fire
walk out of the warmth
stand in the night
looking up

This is a cold country

. . .

Touching a tree
I become
a tree

Watching a deer
I become
a deer

walking
to the
saltlick

If I lift a gun
I am
the dying

If I watch
I am the taste
right
on the tongue

. . .

The doe
hesitates
then walks
out into the meadow

White
reveals her

But my eyes
protect her

I can take the bucket
fill it with tracks
of her small
hooves
bring them to the stove
I feed
parts of trees
I live

I live in the cup of the poem

THE CUP OF THE BEAR

I

I have been driving
North
since noon.

A white line
pulls me.

I follow that white line

and The Bear.

II

A relative said, once,
to a child: look for
The Bear and find

The Star — you will always
know
your way home.

III

And The Big Dipper
stays there.

It scoops that liquid dark
into a dark cup.

It holds this vessel up
to the mouth of
The North.

Drink.   Drink.

I start somewhere
until directions
find me.

IV

Where the river breaks into
white,
falling, you say:
I went to hunt The Bear.

But the orbit of the earth
threw me.

I stood alone beside
The Cross.
Altar and Triangle
mocked me.

I wanted to hold the animals
in my arms: The Lion, The Hare
— like this.

V

Let this be the last poem of
the cup.

Let everything flow together
in one river
and call that river
Kalix.

Traveller, if you go as far North
as you can, you come to the mouth
of this river.

This is where you came to wash.

This is where you bent to drink.

VI

The Big Dipper was floating
in the vat of the heavens,
when I walked
to Helge's house.

Helge took a small dipper,
skimmed some cream off the vat:
Here, child.

Then he took a big dipper
and filled my bucket
with milk.

The constellation lost
its cup
and found
the larger shape
of The Bear.

That chased me.   To run
and stop,
where I could see the light
from Helge's house,
by the milky way
of the snow-
covered river.   I looked up.

The North touched the handle of
The Little Dipper
that poured
into the Big
Dipper.

VII

Some night when The North
is heavy in me
I take the infant to the window
hold her high above my head
and say. This is your cup.

And when the buds of the twin-star
magnolia are covered
with ice,
I will take my son
by the hand
and walk, past the rowen-tree.

I will name the animals: The Bull.
The Bear.   I will tell him
of the twin stars in the handle of
The Big Dipper
and how to find his way
home.

And he will stand there,
inheritor of space,
looking for his seven
sisters.

VIII

I am a pilot
in a small plane,
on some unlit airstrip,
lifting
to that dark.
The daylight
that shuddered in my wings
does not scare me, for I will arc upward
into such a familiar
space
that I will laugh
and know
my sister.

IX

Grandfather came, from death,
to sit beside me.

I told him: the word that is the name
of the river, Kalix,
is the word for
chalice.

I found the meaning in a book
that opened by itself.

But grandfather was silent.
He was looking at the river,
and the river was
light.

X

I went to the blind woman
to ask her
for visions.

I looked into her eyes.
But all I saw was my face
and my hands
that are cups.

Like deer in the woods
they are looking for
water.

This is my exile:

to walk
from country to country
North
to the cup of The Bear.

XI

These two that we are:
the twin I imagined
somewhere in space
and I, on earth, both
travellers to water,
we meet by the river.

You come to me tired;
I give you my hands.
You tell me of hunting;
I fill them with water.

XII

Once I held a stone
in the space of each
hand.

One stone was white,
the moon's sister.

The other was dark, a fossil.
I broke it open, gave you
half
remember this,
when you place your part
of this my dark
stone
next to the white
stone.

II. HANDS

Once I told my shadow to fall
down the face of a cliff,
but it would not
go alone.

It holds on to the sole
of my foot, calculating
each step.   It's high noon.
It has been high noon too long now.

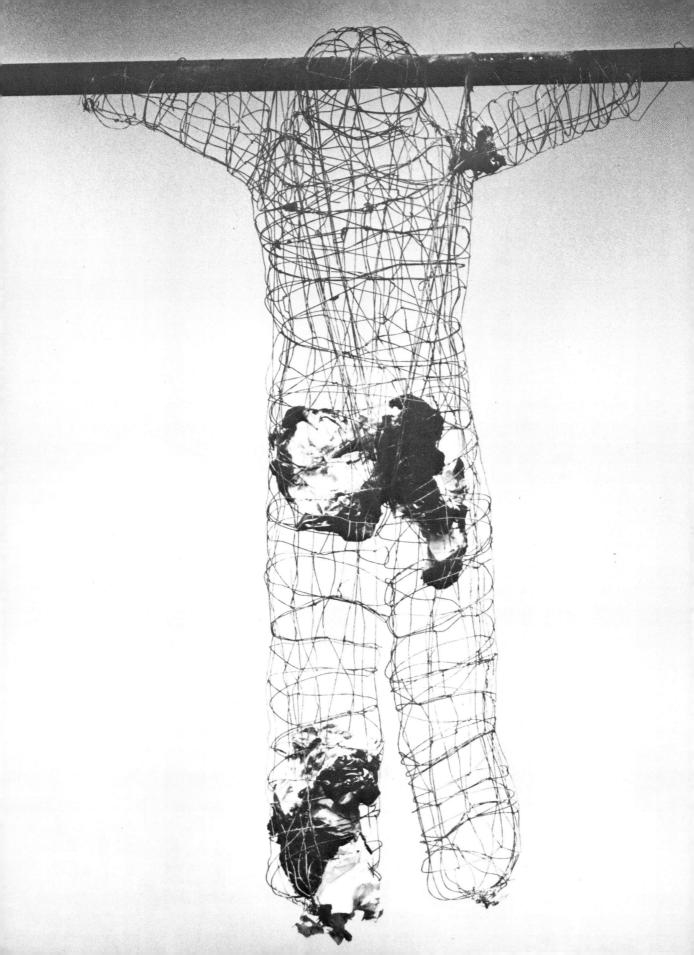

HANDS

I

When I fall asleep
my hands leave me.

They pick up pens
and draw creatures
with five feathers
on each wing.

The creatures multiply.
They say: "We are large
like your father's
hands."

They say: "We have
your mother's
knuckles."

I speak to them:
"If you are hands
why don't you
touch?"

And the wings beat
the air, clapping.
They fly

high above elbows
and wrists.
They open windows
and leave

rooms.
They perch in treetops
and hide under bushes
biting

their nails.   "Hands,"
I call them.
But it is fall

and all creatures
with wings
prepare to fly
South.

II

When I sleep
the shadows of my hands
come to me.

They are softer than feathers
and warm as creatures
who have been close
to the sun.

They say: "We are the giver,"
and tell of oranges
growing on trees.

They say: "We are the vessel,"
and tell of journeys
through water.

They say: "We are the cup."

And I stir in my sleep.
Hands pull triggers
and cut
trees. But

the shadows of my hands
tuck their heads
under wings
waiting
for morning,

when I will wake
braiding

three strands of hair
into one.

THERE IS A GAME WE USED TO PLAY:

I take your fingers: the fish
is caught. Draw a circle
on your skin
around your wrist: the head
is cut. One of my nails
scratches a narrow line
up your inner arm: the belly's
slit. All my fingers flutter
near that slit: the intestines
are out. One of my fingers is
a knife, that moves, quick and
hard, until all scales are off.
Then my hands stroke up and down
— water, rinsing: the fish is clean.
Spread some butter on,
some salt. Pepper, Parsley.
Salt the belly. Put your arm,
then, in the fire. Let it cook.

I take the fingers of the other
hand (there is a game) chop the
head off (we used to play) slit
the belly, throw the intestines
to the dog (to please our senses)
rinse you clean, prepare you for
the fire.

RADAR

We were caught in a cloud.
Icing conditions.
"Look at the cap of the fuel tank,"
you said, "there you can see the ice
form."

And I looked as if my looking
would stop the icing
that had started to change
the shape of the wing,
to alter airflow
and lift
to weigh us
down.

Our instruments were dead.

I went to radar school.

Flight after flight I sit
and stare at the scope.
I like the movement of the dial,
the steady going back
and forth. Clocklike. Heartbeat.

THE SWALLOW

Its black and white formality
was laid on grass and wildflowers
in a shoe box, was carried
up the hill to the church yard,
was buried
by the headstone of a lost relation.

My children bury the fieldmouse,
the robin, the chipmunk.
They place a cross on the grave.
They are not
Christians.

A cardinal hits my windshield.
There is an explosion of red.
My son calls from his nightmare:
"The red moon is coming
with a purple light
to fill my room . . ."

Even the breathing
of a sleeper beside me
cannot help me
when the red moon comes.   "Father,
the dead shall ride out of their
graves."   I fasten my spurs.   I mount.

ICE

While we were sleeping
the ice came.

It covered each branch,
roof,
walk,

and every blade of grass
had its own icicle
growing upward
from the lawn.

I sucked the ice
on the tips of branches.

I slipped my gloved fingers
over fences, pines,
the thickened shapes
of leaves.

And I showed my guests
these gardens.

A branch broke,
and another.

A tree snapped,
and
another.

What could we do —
spend the night, outside,
holding up those old
lilacs?

Or, with a candle,
try to melt the space around
each petrified
bud?

And we fell asleep
thinking of ice
around clocks,
still ticking,

ice in the shape of cups
and covering
tables . . .

and us, in our beds:
sheets and flowering
pillowcases,

how perfectly the ice
would curve
around nostrils
and half-parted lips,

the exposed breast, ice nipple,
hair held in its
flowing,

genitals in that
transparent
cold,

and our fingers,
holding our sleep,
frozen like the tips
of branches.

THE HORSES

The horses that wake me
walk slowly
straining their long loads,

and something of death and
my father
pulls me to see again

grandfather's mare and
the sled,
heavy up the hill in snow,

pulling an infant brother
to burial
on the mountain.

In my father's workshop
there was
an orange can of glue

with two horses perpetually
pulling
in opposite directions —

something I stared at
to understand.
They are working horses,

and they keep pulling.

AWAKENING

Whatever I have forgotten
travels down my fingers.

The raindrops have such small windows.
I open the doors in my nails.

THE QUESTION

Hands reach,
straight arms pull deep
through water, leap
through air,

belly hollowed by
each reach;
feet flutter,
eyes blur aqua.

I measure
nine strokes per lap
for twenty laps,
then I turn on my back

reaching for the certainty
of water behind me,
I swim under poplars
and the summer gum tree's

red hint of autumn.
I could drown,
a bat in the water,
a fish in a tree —

or continue this measuring
stroke by stroke
guaranteed accurate
like an underwater clock.

ISLANDERS

The landscape is the same wherever we go;
the snow is melting.
Green hills demand a rocky shore;
more dunes gather.

What can we do?   All directions are the same.
The water draws
the limit. We know
of differences: the seasons, a catch of fish,
genitals exposed behind the bedroom door.

But we wear the similarities: overalls,
questions to the weather, an unchanging
countenance.

Permanence scares us. We tear the pages,
build a fire, leave the room, turn a corner
in the town.

Down where the road ends, we stand
and talk about delays:
the spring, the storm, the ferry.

ARCHITECTURE IN WHITE

1.

I construct
white rooms
around me:

white walls,
white ceilings,
white floors.

I walk from room
to room.
I handle things.

2.

On a windowsill
there is a chambered
nautilus, cut,
cross-sectioned.
I follow the curve
of its spiral,
chamber to white
chamber to
center.

3.

In the center of worlds
there are white cities,
I have travelled

and stopped where the white
buildings are heavy
holding on, to earth.

And sometimes in dreams
there are cities of mirrors
where I run. My image

merges
with window displays:
I have a thousand hands

without elbows and shoulders,
hands that hold
only gloves.

I am the mannequin
with vacant rooms
in my eyes.

THE ART OF DYEING

If we had pomegranates, we would use pomegranates.
I follow the directions to dye, to darken the color,
to obtain black. What mordant should I use?

I look for the leaves of lily-of-the-valley,
search the woods for shoots of fern, open each
crocus, for saffron. Lichen is most easily cut
from the rocks after rain. There is skin to be
boiled and bark to be soaked. I use rain water,
when possible.

Dyeing is difficult. What plant is appropriate?
(If we had pomegranates, we would use pomegranates)
I want to dye red. Madder.

THE THREE STAGES OF THE SEA

I

the three stages of the sea
and still within the dream
I start to name —

The first: the place
where moon and sea are
one, under the taut belly's
skin.

The second?
and I am trying to recall
a word that I must spell.
Waves. Undulations. Or

embrace. The third?
And all is blank.

II

And from my lazy nap at noon
I wake and walk into the sea.
Far from winters I have come
to dive into this green.
No bird or wood

could wear the color of this coral
reef or fish, purple fans
I try to pick, starfish — orange,
urchin — red, sunrise tellin.
And when my eyes

are done with sight,
and feet are numb from being
fin, I swim my catch of color in,
to let it dry, to wrap it up,
to bring it North.

III

And now I sit
with my small catch
observing it.

The purple fans
are palest mauve.

Seastar and urchin
both are white,

and the small skull
of coral in my hand

has no more color now
than bone.   Siv, I say,

there is no way
to get away from your

landscape, and yours is
snow — bone, coral brain

and winter skin —
that left a native sea

to loose all color here.
White is number three.

RESCUE
(a letter)

I

I cannot move my feet.
They are covered with blankets.
My feet are a hospital.
The people who crashed in the sea
are rescued and brought
to my feet.
I am told not to move them.
The beds would tumble
and blood-banks.
Nurses. Doctors. Sirens.
Corridors.

II

I sit in bed.
I want to read your poems,
slowly, one by one,
but my son
creates an airport and
a sea. Planes
crash. S.O.S.. Rescue
mission. Radios. Messages punctuated:
"Mamma, look."

               I guess I could have chosen
a more quiet place,
if I could choose.
But I accept
the small god in this child.
He knows no death.   The pillow
is a shore.   He numbers planes
and rescue cars.   All vehicles
and men
get home.

III

It is morning, last day of March,
I write you this:
I am rescued, every day, from
nothingness. On paper after paper
my left-handed son
creates a body, head,
long hair, eyes, nose and
smile. Just this week
the circle of my body was centered:
navel. I sometimes stand
beside a house, that has a door that opens
to an upstairs room. Above the roof,
the cross of a plane
hesitates.

I have no fingers, but my arms
are straight and always
reaching
up. I seem to wait for the day
when some god
will give me
hands. You — from what ocean
would you rescue me, on the day
when wings break and breakers wash
the wings? And when you create
my body on a page, how would you
center me — and give my reaching arms
hands?

FIGURE EIGHTS

My back toward the circle, I skate,
shift my weight, turn toward the center.

The skill is in the balance, the ability
to choose an edge, and let it cut

its smooth line.   The moon is trapped
in the ice.   My body flows

across it.   The evening's cold.   The space
limited.   There is not much room

for hesitation.   But I have learned a lot
about grace, in my thirty-third year.

I lean into the cutting edge: two circles
interlock, number eight drawn

by a child, a mathematician's
infinity.

III. TOUCHING

Help me
with
the buttons.

My body
is
the only clothing
I can possibly
wear.

NOTES FOR A LOVE POEM (I)

put on the coat I wore last winter;

sunflower seeds in the right pocket.

. . .

I have lost the blue mitten
with the red rose

. . .

waking you
often

breakfast:
such a hunger

. . .

I look at my left thumb.

It speaks of being alone.

NOTES FOR A LOVE POEM (II)

both of us know how old these rocks are

where we sit

watching the river

. . .

climbing a mountain

building a fire

cooking some food

. . .

I name the oak, the sumac,
maple, willow, alder, sycamore
— notice the bark —
and the small cones of hemlock

Everything has a name

. . .

The Indians speak of spring water,
well water,
melted snow
and water from the six directions

. . .

father sister son

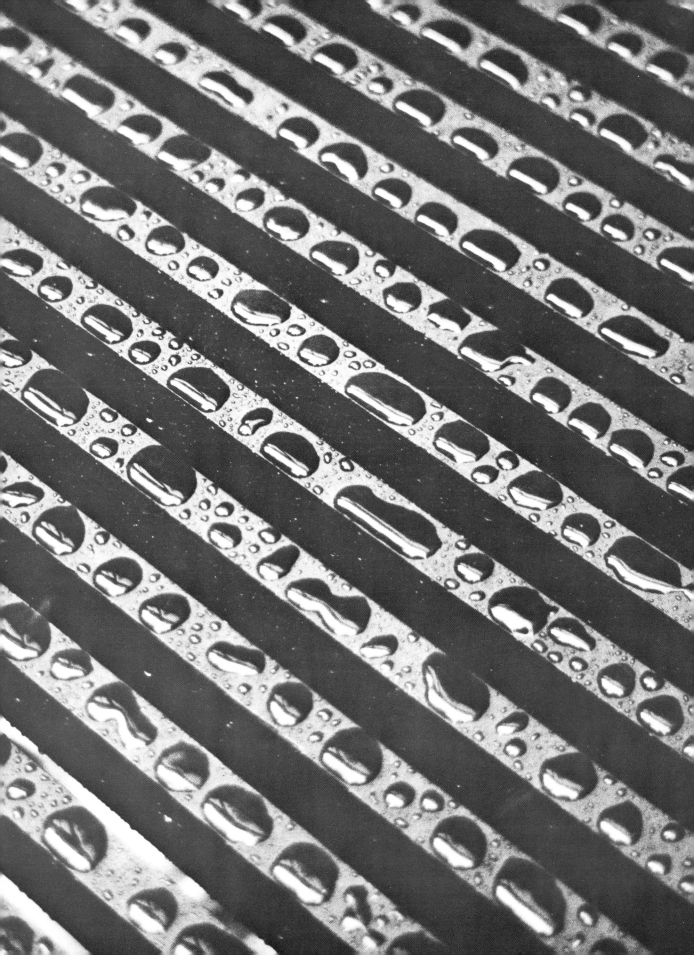

POMEGRANATES

you take me to the woods
where the sun is still warm
on brown leaves
you show me how to squeeze
the fruit
bite a small hole
and suck

fresh water sifted in soil
drawn by roots to rise
in the trunk
to be red and sweet
in the fruit
and yet sweeter
in my mouth
before I give you
to drink

OCTOBER

Fell asleep watching the stars;
The great plow cutting through space.

The back of the stationwagon is a good bed;
Windows all around.

Woke to a light hail;
Snow on the windshield.

And a feeling of you
Keeping me warm in that first cold.

The meadow outside so pale.
The hardwoods on the hill burning.

ORNITHOLOGY

The woodcock rises
in a complicated dance.
The cardinal has color.
The lark has song.
And some small birds
attract their mates
with intricate
constructions.

I brush my hair,
wear bright colors and
French perfume,
and walk around
my garden,

kick a pebble and
pick a rose,
lift the rose up
to my lips
to feel a petal:
penis skin.

WHEN I WAS GODIVA

I

When I was Godiva
with the long hair
ready to ride
the streets in anger,

I cut my hair short.
For bare nipples alone
could not reveal
my nakedness.

II

Before the mirror,
I cover myself with
my hair,
grown long again,

thinking how you will
lift it,
above my shoulders,
and look at me.

MATINS

I

In the small of the morning
I want to wake, to bring you something:
the call of the morning dove,

soft like that
or the light where your shoulder
meets the pillow.

II

If I cannot find flowers, two handfuls
of berries (the bushes scratch my fingers)
or a cup of spring

water, should I return, emptyhanded,
my breasts to fill the cups
of your fingers?

III

I used to sleep late, to wake when the sun
was high as a daughter should be
tall and fair;

now I wake early and know,
writing this poem tells me,
I should bring you the child in the morning.

MAD RIVER

when I flew
over the Mad
River
there was only the sound
of wind
in my wings

> what if I say that sound is visible
> that I have seen it
> travelling across a screen:
> green waves and green
> mountains
>
> and that hands on dials
> control it

my hand on a nob
decided my release
from earth

> I awoke in an upstairs room
> in a farm house, your arms
> around me, small flowers
> were peeling off
> the walls, the bed
> was by the window
>
> Orion had held our sleep
> all night and we woke
> to snow falling,
> falling
> and flowers
>
> we lay there, still,
> the bed would creak,
> there was no sound

I saw my shadow as a cross
touching trees
and water

                              riding
                down a line of light
                through waves
                mountains

                there are hands on dials
                controlling things
                we hear
                no
                silence

                but on either side the trees are standing
                dark
                and under trees the snow is holding
                a thousand cups
                and in each cup
                a shadow
                and in each shadow
                silence

but I knew my body
would bring me down
to trees
water

                and what if I say that
                in writing this poem
                I misspelled a word

                it made the sound of the bed
                into a slit of water
                running

POEM

From what strange country do you come, then?
And do they have horses there?
And swallows?
who slip out of mudbanks and barns
to grow wings in the air.

When I sleep I travel far.

Once I saw the whole sea
run up on shore, and mares
reached me in my sleep
and asked:
Where do you want to go?

If they come again I will say:
Take me to his
country — brook-bed, river-bed
mountain-meadow — where I can be small,
a pebble, and something large like water, wind,
and sun
will hold me.

ZOOLOGICAL GARDENS

1.

If you come with your mother's voice
telling you
of jungles

or your father's hand
teaching you the hunter's
gesture

you might turn away.

2.

If you bring a child to show him
the stripes in fur, the paw,
the mane,

the reason for wings, or horns, or
plumage,
remember, these are gardens:

things must grow here.

3.

Consider the wisdom
of the tiger — all that patience
in his pacing —

and run
through the yellow grasses
waiting

in his eyes.

IV. THE RIVER

*There is an island where only lily-of-the-valley
grows and wild choke cherry.   The farmer who owns
this island burned it once, twice, so that grass
would grow, but only lily-of-the-valley grew and
choke cherry.   Once a boy wanted to go to his grandfather's island.   He started to row across the river.
He knew that on this island only lily-of-the-valley
grew and the white, wild choke cherry blossoms.   But
the river spoke to the boy.   It said: "I come from a
whiter country," and it tipped the boat in the current,
close to the island.   The boy sank in the water.
There was nothing for his hands to hold.*

WHITE AND THE RIVER

I

I am my father.

I go out into the whiteness.
My skis slide their parallel
lines,
and poles alternate
their starprints.

I go to hunt some white thing,
some ptarmigan that lost all color
for this season,
I will hunt her home,
hang her by her feet in the cellar,
where she can spread
her white wings,
while I pull her snowfeathers
off
for the dark roast
she will become
on the white cloth

of my Sunday table.

— or some ermine,

regal white weasel
with the black tail tip,

I will catch
and kill,

strip the skin off
to reveal the smell.

Kings and Queens are
little girl dreams.

— or a hare
will leap

shot.

II

And I am my brother.
I walk with my father
by the river.

We shall cross the river.
We know the ice is
thin.

I say:
"If you fall in
I will let you drown.

I will not pull you up.
I will push you
in."

And he looks at me,
and we walk, together,
out on the ice

that cracks,
but holds,
and cracks.

If he fell in
would he swim
underneath the ice,

groping for a place
where he would find
a breath,

and another,
to surface someplace,
further down river

where the current is harder
and ice cannot hold,
to return,

would he return
to swim in my dream?
— or sink

and lie on the bottom
as I lay
when I was four

and the boat had tipped over,
and my father found me
on the bottom of the river

and pulled me up
so that I can say:

"If you fall in
I will let you drown."

III

And I am my father,
and the boat has tipped over.

I dive for my son
again and
again,

until I see him lying
on the bottom of the river,

arms straight out
and eyes
looking up,

and I dive to his blue eyes
and pull the small body

through water to surface
air and
shore.

IV

And I am my mother,
I wash by the
river.

Boil the sheets
white,
and scrub at the
rugs.

The sun is warm.
It is good by
the river.

Rinse the clothes
clean
to blow dry
in the wind.

And my daughters call me.
"Run.   Mamma.
Run.

The horse has kicked
brother.
The hoof in his
face."

The hoof in his face
while I wash by
the river.

The hoof in his face.

The hoof in his face.

V

Daughter, sister,
girl who picked
flowers,

(I wear a scar
on my face
from the hoof.)

marsh marigold,
the first by
the river,

>"Why did you set
>the furniture
>on fire?"

and bunches of violets
brought home to
mother.

>"Why did you lose
>the nails and
>the screws?"

I lifted the skulls of
cows and
oxen

observing, quite rightly,
that flowers grow
wilder

where bones
had been thrown
from the butchery shop.

VI

And I am my father,
and I stop,
pull an orange from the pocket
and peel it,
throw the peelings on the snow,

pick up my gun
and ski back home,
hang my white killing
on a hook in the cellar
where bloodoranges lie

a crateful
of color
in winter.

NAUTILUS

1

And here
again:
the slice of chambered nautilus,

the absolutely
perfect
spiral, my simple mathematics

cannot
comprehend:
(logarithmic? exponential?)

but I hold it
and travel the curve
to a center, where some mindless

creature
of the sea
began an architecture.

2

I tell my son about
the heavens
and how that cool river
in the sky
is part of a spiral,

how one nebulous arm is
flung, out
in space, and that our
large world
is small, there, somewhere,

where suns and stars move
like drops

in currents

of water.

I hold an imaginary sphere
in my hand: I am the sun.
And he, the world, runs
around me.   Then we stretch
our arms, out, and turn,
slowly, around and around:
two galaxies on the blue
carpet's

limited
space,

and dizzy and laughing
we fall. We feel the pulse
in the river of veins.
"The universe pulsates,"
I say, "expands, contracts,
and they say it's
saddle shaped."

3

One night
there will be
horses

and my son will be
one
of the riders

riding
to that cool
river.

The horses will reach
their long
necks

to drink.
The drinking
will fracture

the surface of
stars, sliver
the moon,

circle upon
circle
growing

outward.

I am a rider.
My love is a rider.
My daughters and
my son.

RIVER AND LIGHT

I

I sit in the marsh-
light that is golden
from midnight sun,
from tufts,
cotton grass,
cloud berries.

I sit
hunched
behind a dwarfed
pine,

And I see the female moose
and her calf
walk out
into the light
of the marsh.

She lifts her head.
The long ears listen.
The nostrils read
the inhabitants of the wind.

But the wind comes my way.
Undetected
I remain
locked in my human
smell.

And the female moose
and her calf
bend to drink.

The water is rusty with iron
and rainbowed from standing
still between tufts.

The rainbows
stir,
yield to the drinking,
flow in under
velvet nostrils,
to be iron in the hump of the calf,
horn in his crown
and marshlight in the eye of the moose.

I drowse.

A buzzing in my ears
and my eyes open.
I see the heads of the cottongrass
letting go,
gathering,
rising,

the spirit of each waterhole
deserting its body
to ghost
over the marsh,
Christ on the churchwall
ascending.

And I drowse,

until an axe
starts to split morning.
I shiver.   Rise.
Walk out of the marsh.

II

Once I rode naked on logs
set in their journey
to sawmill
and sea.

I ran out in the water,
caught them in the current,
climbed up and laughed
as they rolled and dunked me
in the river,

to cling, to climb up again,
to float, down-
stream,
arms out, balancing.

And I swam ashore
when I saw the boys
come down to the river,
to strip their clothes off,
to stand, straight as saplings and
slender, hands
hiding genitals, before
that first plunge
into water.

For I had thought about being
that water.
When my body began to curve
like a river,
I loosened my hair and
floated, head first,
the long hair diffusing around me,
strange undulations,
seagrass,
nipples like pebbles.

Soon as wide in the belly
as the river in spring,
swelling,
covering islands and
willows,
I think about death that is only
water
in lungs, fish and gill
floating down-
stream,
the river wide
after thawing.

III

Sweet Christ in the morning!
Is there no ultimate
baptismal?

when your belly carries its own
seas,
where some small being
moves through evolutions?

when you wear your mother's dream
of the white bride
and your father's dream
of the bride of Christ?

When you have been patient
in temporary churches,
tents risen to the new
evangelist: "Come.
Come to Christ.   Let Jesus wash . . .
Be purified
in water."

When nothing inside you answered?

I climbed the birchtree,
innocent observer
of bathers and
rowers,
and a white bull was led
and a cow waited,
the cloved monster clumsy on her back,
down,
hit,
hoofs on white hide,
down,
hit,
the long carrot-thing protruding,
up again
and in.

And I climbed the stairs
to the abortionist.

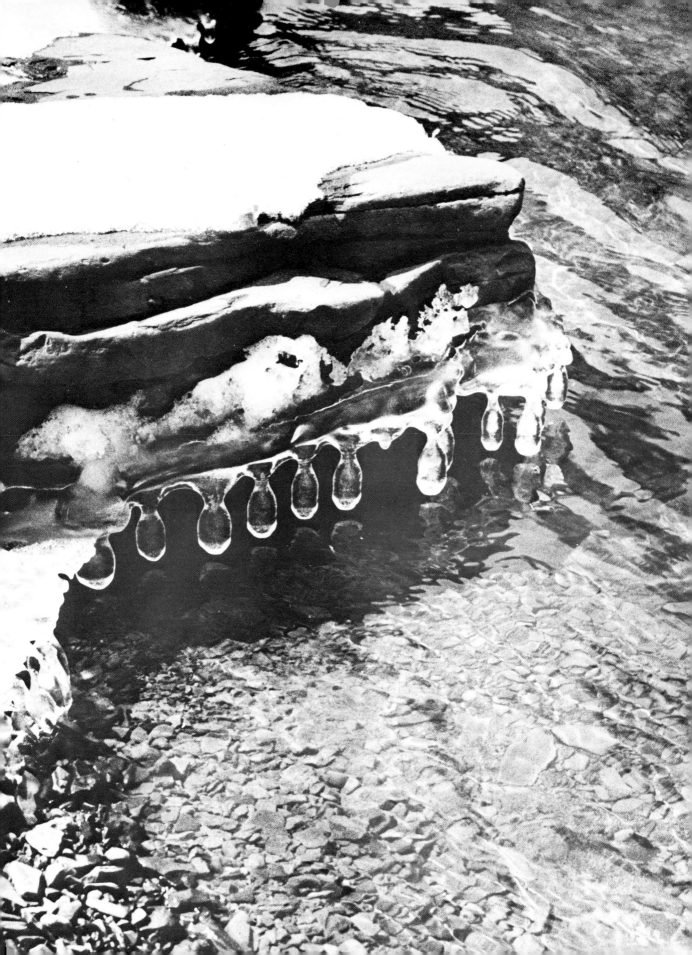

IV

But the river—

In early spring
the ice tugs at sandbar
and rock.
Blocks tear
loose,
mad with the weight of
winter
and logs
that someone has axed
or screamed electric saws through,
stripped clean of branches,
brought to the river,
trees
slender as boys
and waiting
for ice-break

Stirs,

and I know
it is not to be
the blood of the lamb
but the blood of a woman
when all her rivers let go
and from her own sea
the child comes, the small face
wise as the three kings
and with all
their giving.
And in some room, golden
with morning
and moose-light
something would have to break free.

Daughter, what do I give you?